30p

Tommy and the

Grimace says

THIS BELONGS TO

claire willow

McDonald's

Tommy and the
island

CONTENTS

1 *Tommy and the new bridge*

Tommy the Tugboat works very hard. He is always willing to guide a liner or a cargo ship, to tow an oil rig or help a fishing boat. But, each summer, Robert, his captain takes him for a holiday.

Tommy gets very excited. Every morning for weeks, he asks: 'Have you decided where we are going, Robert?'

But this year, Robert couldn't make up his mind. He studied his maps and charts. His friend, Walter, the gate-keeper at Spedemouth Docks, suggested many interesting places. But Robert didn't really want to go to any of them.

The morning before they were due to leave, Walter came along the dock wall pushing a hand-truck. On it was a large crate.

'Good-morning, Walter,' called Robert. 'That looks heavy.'

'It is,' panted Walter. 'It's an engine for my Uncle Ben's boat. I'm taking it to the railway station.'

'Uncle Ben!' repeated Robert. 'From Wales! He owns the boat yard at Aberford.'

'That's right,' said Walter.

'I remember him,' said Tommy. 'He mended me a few years ago.'

'He remembers you, too,' chuckled Walter. 'You saved his boat yard.'

Walter explained that Uncle Ben needed a new engine for his launch, but he couldn't afford to buy a new one. Walter had bought a good second-hand one for him. He was sending it off by train to Aberford.

'I only hope it will arrive safely and quickly,' added Walter. 'Aberford is already full of visitors who want Uncle Ben to take them on fishing trips.'

'That's how I'd like to spend my holiday,' said Robert.

'Then why don't we go to Aberford again?' asked Tommy. 'I enjoyed being there last time. I had lots of adventures. We could take the engine to Uncle Ben.'

8

'A grand idea!' cried Robert. 'We'll set out to-morrow.'

The engine was loaded aboard. Walter went off to telephone Uncle Ben. Robert hosed down Tommy's deck. He cleaned the red band round his white funnel, and the scarlet tyres that stopped Tommy bumping into the dock wall. He checked his fishing rods, and stocked up with tins of food.

Early next morning, Walter turned the big wheel. The dock-gates swung open, and Tommy chugged through.

'Goodbye,' called Walter. 'Best wishes to Uncle Ben. Have a happy holiday.'

'Toot-toot,' tootled Tommy.

He chugged down the river to the sea. It was a long journey to Aberford, but the weather was perfect. Tommy and Robert enjoyed themselves. First, they chugged southwards, and then west-wards along the busy English Channel. Sometimes, Tommy stopped for a few hours so that Robert could fish. Sometimes, they stayed the night in a seaside harbour. Robert went ashore to buy fresh bread and newspapers.

9

They reached Land's End, where the green ocean rollers pounded on rocks. Tommy tootled to the lonely lighthouse. Then Robert steered him northwards towards Aberford. Tommy was chugging along over the rumbling, tumbling blue sea, when he heard a hooting sound.

A large tugboat was steaming up behind him. As it drew level, Tommy could hear its engines throbbing and thumping. The name 'Trout' was painted on its bows.

'Ahoy there, Trout!' called Tommy. 'Where are you going in such a hurry?'

'Can't waste time answering questions,' retorted Trout. 'I'm needed in the Haven to finish building a bridge.'

'Building a bridge!' exclaimed Tommy. 'How can a tugboat build a bridge?'

But Trout was already way ahead of him.

'That's very odd!' said Robert. 'I wonder what he meant.'

As Tommy chugged northwards, the weather began to change. The sun disappeared. Storm clouds raced in from the west. The wind moaned around his mast. The sea turned from blue to angry grey.

Tommy was a sturdy tugboat. He was used to rough weather. But, as the hours passed, a gale blew up. He was tossed from one white-topped wave to the next. Green water rolled along his deck. Squalls of rain and spray beating against his cabin windows almost blinded him. Robert had a hard job holding him on course. Even with Tommy's engines running at full power, he was travelling very slowly.

This was very lucky for Trout. Otherwise, Tommy could never have seen him in time. As Tommy chugged around a headland, there was the other tugboat dead ahead. Robert wrenched at the wheel. Tommy swung sideways.

'Blistering Barnacles!' exclaimed Tommy. 'That was a near thing!'

'Tommy! Tommy!' called Trout. 'Help me!'

'What's the trouble?' tootled Tommy.

'My steering gear has broken,' shouted Trout. 'I shall be driven on to the rocks or the beach. Please help me!'

'I'll try,' promised Tommy.

First, Robert fired a rocket carrying a line across Trout's deck. This line was fastened to a thicker rope, and the rope was fastened to Tommy's strong cable. The sailors on Trout hauled aboard the thin line, the thicker rope, and then the cable. They made the cable fast to Trout's bows. Tommy started to tow.

But the plunging, helpless Trout was wallowing and bucking. The cable snapped!

Once again, Robert fired the rocket, and managed to fasten another cable to Trout. Once again, Tommy began to pull. The cable snatched and tightened.

'Stop, Tommy!' hooted Trout. 'The cable will break again.'

'I can't tow in this storm, Robert,' cried Tommy. 'Trout is too heavy.'

'I know you can't,' said Robert. 'Just hold him steady in this bay until morning. Perhaps the gale will blow out.'

There was no sleep for anyone that night. Tommy needed all his strength to stop them both being driven on to the beach. But, by early morning, the storm clouds were blowing away, and the pale sun rose. Robert listened to the weather forecast on his radio, and checked his charts.

'Ahoy there, Trout!' he called. 'The storm is over. We're about sixty kilometres from the Haven. Tommy will try and tow you there.'

'Thank you very much, Tommy,' said Trout.

Tommy was small, but he had a very strong engine. The wind was blowing towards the Haven, and the sea had calmed down. They passed the entrance to the narrow creek that led to Aberford. Three hours later, they chugged between the buoys that marked the safe channel into the Haven.

'Can you please take me to the Haven Shipbuilding Dock?' asked Trout.

Tommy towed Trout in beside a solid stone jetty. Three other tugboats were moored there. They were called Tarpon, Turtle and Tortoise.

'Where have you been, Trout?' called Tarpon. 'You should have arrived last night. We're waiting to finish the bridge.'

'I wouldn't have arrived at all if Tommy hadn't rescued me,' answered Trout. 'My steering gear is broken.'

'Engineer Joe is going to be very angry,' said Turtle. 'Here he comes now.'

A man wearing a bright orange helmet ran along the jetty.

'You've arrived at last,' he called. 'We must get started straight away.'

'I can't work today,' said Trout. 'I need a repair.' He explained to Engineer Joe all about the accident.

'Now what are we going to do?' cried Joe. 'We're all ready to finish the bridge. But we must have four tugboats.'

'I'm a tugboat,' cried Tommy. 'Can't I help?'

'You're rather small,' said Joe doubtfully.

14

'But he's very strong,' explained Trout.

'Well, we can't wait for another tugboat,' said Joe. 'So if you'll do your best, Tommy . . .'

'He always does that,' promised Robert.

Joe explained that a road bridge was being built high over the Haven. The engineers had constructed some tall pillars in the water. A span of road had been laid on these from each bank. Now the middle span had to be set into place to link up the bridge.

'Why do you want tugboats?' asked Tommy.

'The middle span has been made in this dock-yard,' explained Joe. 'The tugboats will tow it up to the bridge and it will be lifted from the water.'

'That's an unusual way of building a bridge,' said Robert.

'It's the first time it has been tried, so it's very exciting,' said Joe. 'I only hope it works. Are you ready, Tommy?'

'Aye, aye, sir,' tootled Tommy.

'Then come to the front with me,' said Tarpon. 'Turtle and Tortoise are strong, but they're rather slow. They like to work behind things.'

The huge span of bridge was floating near the

entrance of the dock basin. Tarpon and Tommy fastened their cables to the front, and eased it carefully out. Then Turtle and Tortoise fastened their cables to the back.

Very gently and slowly, the four tugboats moved the bridge span up the Haven. They passed the tall towers and the long jetties of the oil refineries.

Ahead, Tommy could see the enormous pillars of the new bridge. From each side of the Haven, a length of roadway, with a crane on the end of it, ran out high over the water. But, in the centre, nothing!

The tugboats towed the bridge span in exactly below this gap. The tide swirled around them as they fought to keep it steady.

'Hold tight, Tommy!' panted Tarpon. 'It mustn't move!'

The cables rattled down from the powerful cranes on the bridge. Men quickly fastened them to the middle span. The four tugboats waited. Everyone was very quiet. There was only the throbbing of the tugboat engines, the rattle of the cables, the grating noise of the cranes, and an occasional shouted order from Joe and his engineers. Little by little, the immense span rose from the water.

The tugboats stood by hour after hour. Darkness came. Arc lights were switched on. Tommy watched the massive middle span hanging in the air above him. Suppose it slipped! But Joe and his men knew their business. Three metres . . . two metres . . . one metre . . . the span was up! With barely a centimetre to spare, it was in place. Carefully, the supports, the rivets and the bolts were fastened. As the sun rose, the bridge was linked.

Everyone cheered and shouted. The tankers hooted. The tired tugboats tootled. Then they chugged slowly down the Haven.

As they were passing one of the long refinery jetties, a man with a loud hailer called from the deck of a giant oil tanker moored there.

'Ahoy there, Tommy! Can you come alongside please?'

As Robert steered Tommy in beside the ship, he could see a tall man wearing a long white robe and head-dress on the deck.

'Hello, Tommy and Robert,' called the man. 'Do you remember me?'

'Sheik Abdullah!' exclaimed Robert. 'You came to Aberford when we were last there.'

'You did me a great service,' called the Sheik. 'Can you do another please? May I charter you both for about twelve days?'

'We were going to Aberford on holiday,' ex-

18

plained Robert. 'What did you want us to do?'

The Sheik explained that his twelve-year-old son Hassin was at school in England. The boy had been so homesick that he had made himself ill. The doctor had suggested a sea voyage. So the Sheik had arranged that they would travel home to Saudi Arabia together in one of his giant oil tankers.

'But there is one problem,' continued the Sheik. 'His school breaks up next Wednesday. I have to fly to America for two weeks. Can you take care of Hassin until I return, and bring him to this Haven to meet me?'

'No need for chartering,' chuckled Robert. 'He can spend a holiday in Aberford with us. What school is he at? I'll telephone his Headmaster and ask him to put Hassin on the train to Penbryn Junction. I'll meet him.'

'Allah will smile on you for your kindness,' said Sheik Abdullah. 'We'll meet again in two weeks' time. Thank you, Robert and Tommy.'

Tommy chugged out of the Haven, on to the tumbling blue and white sea. Robert steered him towards Aberford.

'Now we can start our holiday,' he chuckled. 'A quiet time for you, Tommy. Fishing for Hassin and me.'

'I wonder,' thought Tommy to himself. He knew that adventures had a way of happening to him, especially when he least expected them.

2   Tommy and the Island

A few hours later, Tommy chugged between the two steep headlands, and up the deep narrow creek that led to the village of Aberford. The two old-fashioned inns, the car park and the stone cottages looked exactly as they had when last he saw them.

As he tied up at the stone jetty beside the boat shed, Uncle Ben and all his old friends came on to the quay to meet him. They *were* pleased to see him. Uncle Ben was delighted with the engine.

As soon as lunch was over, Uncle Ben rowed the launch alongside. Robert winched down the engine. They spent the rest of the day fixing it into the launch.

Next day was the monthly market day in Aberford. Tommy saw the cattle trucks rumbling into the car park at the other end of the quay. Soon, there were pens filled with baa-ing sheep, and mooing cows. Beside them, farmers in tweed caps and leather leggings calmed frightened Welsh ponies.

Robert strolled along to watch the auctioneer selling the animals. Uncle Ben was busy outside his boat shed. A man carrying a brief case came along the quayside.

'I'm Mr Percy, from the Welsh Folk Museum,' he said to Uncle Ben. 'I want to go to Gannet Island. I understand that a Mr James lives there. He makes harps.'

'You mean old Brother James,' said Uncle Ben. 'He's lived in the farmhouse on Gannet Island for years.'

'He's one of the best harp makers in Wales,' said Mr Percy. 'Beautiful tone and fine workmanship. How can I reach Gannet Island?'

Uncle Ben scratched his head. 'My new engine hasn't been tested yet. Passage to Gannet Island is pretty rough.'

'Can't I go?' asked Tommy eagerly. 'I'd like to see Gannet Island.'

'Tootle your tooter, and call Robert,' said Uncle Ben.

22

Robert agreed to take Mr Percy out to the island.
Uncle Ben decided that he would go to show them
the way. In a few moments, Tommy was chugging
down the deep narrow creek.

Gannet Island was only about three miles from
Aberford. But it was a dangerous journey. The sea
foamed and swirled around hidden reefs and rocks.
Tommy had to be very careful to keep between the
bell buoys that marked the safe channel.

As they came nearer to the island, they could see
thousands of sea birds. Guillemots and razorbills

rested on the high cliffs, gulls wheeled and glided in the sky, calling and screeching.

'Look, Mr Percy!' cried Robert suddenly. 'Gannets!'

Tommy looked up. Several huge white birds with long pointed beaks were circling high above the water. As he watched, one of them dived like an arrow into the water beside him.

Tommy was so startled that he didn't see the extra big wave. It curled towards him and swept him towards a jagged rock.

'Full speed astern!' yelled Uncle Ben.

Tommy's engines raced, dragging him back from disaster.

'Blistering Barnacles!' he gasped. 'That was a near one!'

Ahead, in a narrow bay, Tommy could see a short concrete jetty. Very carefully, Robert eased him in beside a small motor-boat that was moored there. Tethered to a post on the jetty was a bleating nanny-goat.

Along the jetty and up a steep rocky track to the top of the cliff, ran a pair of lines like a narrow rail-

way. Half-way down the track, a white-bearded man was struggling with a billy-goat.

'Come and give me a hand with this stubborn creature,' he roared. 'I'll never get to market today.'

Robert, Uncle Ben and Mr Percy hurried along the jetty, and up the track. They heaved and pushed. The man tugged. Between them, they managed to get the goat down the track and along the jetty.

The old man wiped his forehead on a red hand-kerchief. 'Lucky for me you happened along. Have you come to see the gannets?'

25

'No,' replied Mr Percy. 'If you're Brother James, I've come to see you. My name is Percy. I'm from the Welsh Folk Museum. We'd like to buy one of your harps.'

'Sorry, I haven't time to talk about it now,' said Brother James. 'Must get these goats to Aberford Market. I have to sell all my animals. I'm leaving the island on the first of August. I'm going to Canada. Too old to live here alone any more.'

'Will anyone else come and live on the island?' asked Robert.

'I don't know,' answered Brother James. 'I rent it. Now it's to be sold at an auction sale at the Lobster Pot Inn at Aberford on Saturday the seventeenth of July at three o'clock.'

'I'd like to own an island,' said Robert.

'Will you give me a hand to load these goats into my boat please?' asked Brother James. 'I shall have to make four trips to take just my herd of goats to market.'

'I could take them all in one trip,' suggested Tommy.

'That would be kind of you,' said Brother James.

'Could you manage some sheep and a pig too?'

'Yes, of course,' replied Robert.

It took nearly two hours to drive the goats and the pig down to the jetty. The sheep were brought down, one at a time, on a little truck which ran on the lines. There was a rope fastened to the back of the truck, and around a sort of capstan at the top of the cliffs. As Brother James's pony Flora walked around the capstan, it turned, winding the rope and drawing the truck up the cliff. Turned the opposite way, it let the truck down slowly and safely.

When the animals were loaded, Tommy looked like Noah's ark. There were goats tethered to his rails, sheep penned behind his cabin, and a pig on his fore-deck. Everyone was hot and tired, so Brother James suggested that they should go up to the farmhouse for a cup of coffee. He would show Mr Percy his harps.

It was then that Tommy noticed the old quarry to the left of the track, part way up the cliff. The stone had been cut away, leaving a flat grass-covered space. On this, was a ring of man-sized rock pillars. Each was carved into a statue.

'What are those statues?' asked Tommy, when everyone came back to the jetty.

'My friends!' chuckled Brother James. 'I've carved twelve of them in the past thirty years to keep me company. Pity I shall have to leave them behind.'

'Who are they?' asked Uncle Ben.

'My Round Table,' answered Brother James. 'I've carved some of the knights of King Arthur's Round Table, and King Arthur himself. He's nearest the track.'

28

Mr Percy went back up the track and studied the statue of King Arthur.

'This is magnificent!' he exclaimed. 'These statues should be preserved in the Welsh Folk Museum. Because, although no one really knows where King Arthur lived, there are rocks and caves named after him all over Wales. So we like to think he was a Welsh Prince.'

'And I'm a Welsh sculptor, and these are carved out of Welsh rock on a Welsh Island,' chuckled Brother James.

'I'm sure the Museum would buy them from you,' said Mr Percy.

'I wouldn't sell my friends!' declared Brother James. 'And, anyway, how could they be taken to Aberford? They're very heavy. They'd sink my little boat.'

'A great pity,' sighed Mr Percy. 'We could set out a Round Table garden. Everyone would come to see them.'

'Come along, Mr Percy,' called Robert. 'Otherwise, the market will be over before we reach Aberford.'

Robert started Tommy's engines, and reversed him away from the jetty.

'Goodbye,' called Brother James. 'I'll touch up the varnish on the harp you chose, Mr Percy.'

'Excellent!' cried Mr Percy.

It was afternoon when Tommy reached Aberford. Mr Percy went away in his car. The farmers helped unload the pig, goats and sheep. The auctioneer sold them. When the market was over, the trucks drove away, and the farmers went home. Robert went up to the village.

The harbour was quiet again, except for the squeak of Uncle Ben's saw, as he cut planks outside his boat shed. Tommy had had a busy day. He dozed in the evening sunshine.

3   *Tommy and Martha*

Suddenly, Tommy was awakened by a loud voice shouting, 'Going about!'

An old-fashioned fishing smack was trying to tack down the deep narrow creek. It swung towards the bank, grazing one of the boats moored there.

There were about eight boys milling around on deck. Three of them were pulling on ropes, but the rest were doing nothing.

Uncle Ben dropped his saw, and ran to the quayside.

'Dang old Davy Jones! Some folk are not fit to take a paddle boat on a park lake! Turn her into wind!' he roared.

But the sailing smack kept coming.

'Turn her into wind!' yelled Uncle Ben again.

The fifty-foot sailing smack was a heavy old boat, with large patched tan sails. Tommy knew that if she hit him, even his strong sides could be holed.

'Toot-toot,' he tootled.

Suddenly, the helmsman of the smack saw him. He threw the helm hard over. With a crack of sails, and a rattle of blocks, the smack swung sideways and stopped. The boys on deck tumbled into a heap.

'What do you think you're doing?' shouted Uncle Ben. 'You nearly rammed Tommy.'

The young helmsman came along the deck to the bows. The boys picked themselves up and watched.

'You should learn to sail before you come into narrow creeks,' cried Uncle Ben.

'Sorry, sir,' said the helmsman. 'We usually start our engine and motor into strange harbours. But we have a leaking fuel pipe, so we had to sail in. May we tie up here?'

'Moor beside Tommy,' said Uncle Ben.

'Thank you very much,' said the helmsman. 'My name is Barry. I'm warden of a Birmingham youth club. Our boat is called Martha. She's nearly one hundred years old.'

When Robert came back, Uncle Ben was aboard Martha, trying to mend the fuel pipe. Robert invited the boys aboard Tommy for lemonade and biscuits.

Uncle Ben and Barry climbed up on the jetty, wiping their hands on oily rags.

'It's only a make-shift job,' warned Uncle Ben. 'You need a new fuel pipe. If you have to use the engine, be very careful. There's diesel oil in your bilges.'

'What's a bilge?' asked the oldest boy, whose name was Billy.

'The space under the floorboards in the bottom of a boat,' replied Robert. 'The oil should be cleared out of there as soon as possible.'

'It could be dangerous,' added Uncle Ben.

'How far are you planning to go?' asked Robert.

'We'll sail to the Haven and try and get a new fuel pipe fitted,' replied Barry. 'Then we'll spend the rest of our two weeks holiday cruising.'

Barry and the boys went off to explore Aberford. Robert and Uncle Ben took Uncle Ben's launch down the creek to test the new engine.

'Do you like taking boys for sailing holidays, Martha?' asked Tommy.

'Yes, I do,' replied Martha. 'I'm doing a useful job again. Imagine it, Tommy! Some of these boys had never seen the sea until we left Garnwen.'

Martha explained that, for many years, she had been tied up in a backwater. Then her owner had given her to the youth club so that boys and girls who had never before seen the sea could enjoy sailing holidays. The members had earned the money to paint and repair her by doing odd jobs.

'But, I really need new sails and a better engine,' sighed Martha.

'That would cost a lot of money,' said Tommy.

'I know,' agreed Martha.'

Next morning, Tommy chugged down the deep, narrow creek to the rumbling, tumbling sea. Robert and Uncle Ben were going fishing.

When he was about eight kilometres from Aberford, Robert stopped his engines. The hooks were baited, and the lines cast.

'Look, Robert!' tootled Tommy. 'Isn't that Martha?'

34

The old sailing smack glided past them, tan sails billowing in the light wind.

'She's going very well,' said Robert. 'The boys must be learning fast.'

Robert and Uncle Ben fished until early afternoon.

'The fish aren't biting today,' sighed Robert.

'We'll go towards the Haven and try for mackerel,' suggested Uncle Ben.

The wind dropped. Tommy chugged over a sea as smooth as green glass. Presently, he saw Martha. There wasn't enough wind to fill her sails. She was drifting.

'Ahoy there,' called Tommy. 'Do you want a tow?'

'No, thank you,' answered Martha. 'I'm sure the wind will freshen soon, and we'll reach the Haven.'

'Be careful of the rocky islands called the Cat and Kittens about two kilometres ahead,' warned Uncle Ben. 'The largest island is shaped like a cat. They're especially dangerous after dark.'

'We should be way past them by then,' called Barry. 'Cheerio!'

Uncle Ben steered Tommy around to the other side of the Cat and Kittens.

'This is a good place for mackerel,' he said.

He took two hand lines out of his fishing basket. Each had six bright feathered hooks.

'What bait do we use?' asked Robert.

'None,' replied Uncle Ben. 'Mackerel will chase trailing feathers.'

At the very first cast, Robert had four fish on his line. Exciting hours went by. Tommy's deck was slimy with fish scales. Every bucket, bowl and basket that Robert could find was filled with fish.

'Dang me!' cried Uncle Ben. 'It's nearly nine o'clock. We must start back for Aberford.'

Robert and Uncle Ben stowed the fish and cleaned Tommy's deck. Robert switched on the lights on his masthead. Then he steered Tommy while Uncle Ben cooked four of the tasty fish for supper. It was almost dark.

'Uncle Ben!' called Robert suddenly. 'I can see a light.'

'No one lives on the Cat and Kittens,' said Uncle Ben.

Robert looked through his binoculars. 'What about Gannet Island?'

'We can't see that from here,' replied Uncle Ben. 'Dang me! It's not a light. It's flickering. It's a fire!'

'Martha!' exclaimed Robert. 'Top speed, Tommy. We must go and help them.'

Tommy raced across the sea at top speed. As he drew nearer, he could see that it *was* Martha. Her sails were down. Flames were shooting out of the engine-room hatch. Billy had organised the boys into a bucket chain. They were filling buckets with sea water, and pouring it over the deck and sides to keep them wet, so that they wouldn't burn. Barry was trying to fight the fire with an extinguisher.

'Help me, Tommy,' cried Martha. 'My engine room is on fire.'

'We'll put it out,' tootled Tommy.

Robert steered Tommy in beside Martha. It was lucky that it was so calm. Uncle Ben held Tommy steady, while the boys climbed over Martha's gunwale on to her chain-plates. From there, they could jump on to Tommy's deck. Then they used

Tommy's hose-pipe to keep Martha's sides wet. Robert went aboard Martha with all Tommy's fire extinguishers. He helped Barry fight the fire.

It was hot! Sparks were singeing Tommy's rail. Pieces of burning wood fell on his deck. The boys stamped them out, or threw them into the sea.

At last the flames died down. The fire was out!

'Thank you very much,' said Barry.

'How did it happen?' asked Robert.

'There was no wind to take us to the Haven,'

explained Barry, 'and we were drifting towards those dangerous islands.'

'The Cat and Kittens,' said Uncle Ben.

'Anyway, I decided that I would risk the engine,' continued Barry. 'But it wouldn't start, so that I could see what was wrong, one of the boys was holding an oil lamp when he dropped it. It rolled into the bilges, and the oil must have caught fire.'

Robert fastened Tommy's cable to Martha's bows, and he chugged towards Aberford. Now the danger was over, the boys enjoyed their adventure. Barry cooked two mackerel for each of them. Uncle Ben sat on the hatch cover smoking his pipe, and telling them such exciting stories of whale-hunting and smuggling, that they were almost sorry to reach Aberford.

When the village people heard about the accident, they took the boys back to their houses, gave them hot drinks, and tucked them up in their spare bedrooms. Uncle Ben handed out mackerel to anyone who wanted them. The rest went into the deep freeze at the Lobster Pot Inn.

Martha and Tommy were left beside the jetty.

'Thank you very much, Tommy,' said Martha. 'If you hadn't come along, I'd be at the bottom of the sea now.'

'That's all right, Martha,' said Tommy. 'I'm glad I was there to help. Don't worry. I'm sure you can be mended.'

'But not in time to give the boys their summer holiday afloat,' sighed Martha. 'They'll have to go home.'

'Something is sure to turn up,' said Tommy.

But he hadn't the least idea what that something could be!

4   Tommy rescues Hassin

Next morning, a taxi pulled up on the quay. Robert climbed into it.

'I'll be back by lunch-time, Tommy,' he called. 'Jones the garage is taking me to meet Hassin at Penbryn Junction.'

Uncle Ben and Barry were inspecting the damage to Martha. She needed new deck planking and engine room, and worse still, a new engine! Uncle Ben said that the repairs alone would cost several hundred pounds.

Barry said that Martha wasn't insured, and that all the money the boys had earned with their odd jobs had been spent on Martha already.

'Can't something be done?' asked Tommy.

'If we work hard next winter I'm sure we can earn the money to pay for the repairs,' said Barry. 'But a new engine could be a real problem. In any case, there'll be no more sailing holidays this year. I shall have to hire a mini-bus to take the boys back to Birmingham today.'

'Jones the garage has one,' said Uncle Ben. 'But he's taken Robert to Penbryn Junction to meet the Arab boy, Hassin.'

'Then I'll take the boys beach-combing until lunch-time,' said Barry.

Tommy spent the rest of the morning trying to think up a way to help Martha. She was very upset. She didn't want to be tied up in a backwater again.

At one o'clock, Robert and a dark-skinned boy in grey school uniform, climbed out of the taxi. Jones the garage unloaded several trunks, some flippers and face masks, cricket bats and tennis rackets, and carried them on to Tommy's deck. Then he drove away.

'Hello, Hassin,' tootled Tommy. 'Do you remember me?'

'Hello, Tommy,' said Hassin. 'How long must I wait until my father comes, Robert?'

'About eleven days,' replied Robert.

'It's a long time,' sighed Hassin. 'I don't like England. It's cold. Saudi Arabia is hot and sunny. I want to unpack my books, Robert.'

'Come and have dinner with me,' suggested Uncle Ben. 'Lovely boiled ham, and new broad beans from my garden.'

'No, thank you,' said Hassin. 'I'm not hungry.'

Robert showed Hassin his bunk, and came back on deck.

'There's an unhappy boy,' said Uncle Ben.

'Martha's unhappy, too,' cried Tommy.

He was telling Robert the sad tale when – Phut–Phut–Phut. A small motor-boat chugged up the creek. Brother James was standing in the stern.

Balanced in the bows was a large Welsh harp.

'Ahoy there, Robert!' he called. 'Can you give me a hand?'

Robert and Uncle Ben were struggling to haul the awkward, heavy harp up on to the jetty when Barry and his boys came along the quay. The boys were strong. They lifted the harp, and carried it to the boat shed. Mr Percy would collect it later.

Brother James stood looking down on Martha.

'What happened to her?' he asked.

Barry explained about the fire, and the spoilt sailing holidays. Brother James thought for a moment.

'I'm afraid I can't help Martha,' he said. 'But if your boys are not afraid of hard work, they can have a holiday and help me with a problem.'

'The boys are willing and strong,' said Barry.

'Then bring them to Gannet Island,' suggested Brother James. 'There's room for all of you in my old farmhouse. The island is an exciting place for a holiday. Pirates and smugglers once lived there, and soldiers in the old fort.'

'Hurrah!' cheered the boys.

'Thank you very much,' said Barry. 'What can we do in return?'

'I've been sad at the thought of leaving my statues on the island,' explained Brother James. 'I want your boys to help me move them down to the jetty and—'

'And I'll bring them to Aberford,' interrupted Tommy. 'Please, Robert. I want to help.'

'Of course you can,' chuckled Robert.

The boys were very excited at the idea of a holiday on an island. Hassin came out on deck to watch them and Barry carry all their gear from Martha to Tommy. But he didn't help. Uncle Ben gathered together planks, nails and a power saw to make packing cases so that the statues wouldn't be damaged. Brother James went to telephone Mr Percy about the harp and the statues.

Everyone came aboard Tommy. Barry tied Brother James's small motor-boat to Tommy's stern. Robert started the engine.

'Toot-toot,' tooted Tommy. 'Now don't worry, Martha. We'll think of a plan to help you, too.'

'I do hope so,' sighed Martha sadly.

When Tommy was tied up beside the island jetty, Barry and the boys unloaded their sleeping bags.

'My old pony Flora is grazing up beside the farmhouse,' explained Brother James. 'Leave the heavy gear. She'll bring it up in the morning. Are you coming with us, Hassin?'

'No, thank you, sir,' replied Hassin politely. 'I will stay here with Tommy.'

Next morning, Hassin was reading on Tommy's deck when Barry and the boys came aboard. They told Robert that they had decided to work on the statues in the mornings, and enjoy themselves in the afternoons.

'Where is Brother James?' asked Robert.

'Bringing down Flora,' answered Barry.

Brother James was leading the old pony down the track. She was carrying tools and timber. Barry and Brother James rigged a block and tackle on the jetty. Tommy already had a small lifting crane called a derrick attached to his funnel. It would be quite strong enough to lift one of the statues. His

winch would tug and pull. His engine would give
power to Uncle Ben's saw. Robert and the boys
began to measure and nail.

Everyone was working except Hassin. Flora was
tethered to a mooring post at the end of the jetty.
Hassin climbed up Tommy's gangplank. He walked
along the jetty to where Flora waited. He stroked
her nose and whispered to her. Flora whinnied.
After a while, Hassin climbed on to her back.

'Just look at that,' said Brother James to Robert. 'I wonder if . . . Hassin! Will you bring Flora over here? I need her to move these planks.'

Hassin untied Flora and rode her along the jetty. They worked happily for the rest of the morning. Then he shared his lunch with her.

'You love horses, don't you?' asked Robert.

'Yes,' replied Hassin. 'I have three of my own at home. I've missed them so much.'

'Would you like to look after Flora while you are here?' asked Brother James. 'She likes company, and I shall be very busy.'

'Yes, please,' cried Hassin. 'Can I really take her wherever I like?'

'She must work here in the mornings,' answered Brother James. 'But she shall be your horse for the rest of the day.'

'Thank you,' cried Hassin. 'Perhaps I should sleep at the farm, Robert. Flora will need grooming and feeding and . . .'

'A very good idea!' chuckled Robert.

The next four days were busy ones. Tommy made several trips to Aberford to fetch stores and timber for the packing cases and to deliver statues. Four of them were already standing outside Uncle Ben's boat shed.

Tommy had taken the boys fishing and lifting lobster pots. They had dived, swum, explored rock pools, been bird-watching and had a barbecue. Hassin spent all the afternoons roaming around the island on Flora.

One evening, Tommy was late returning to Gannet Island. When he arrived Brother James hurried down the track.

'Tommy! Robert!' he called. 'Hassin and Flora are missing! No one has seen them since lunch-time. Barry and the boys are out looking for them.'

'Where have you searched?' asked Robert.

'All the bays near here,' replied Brother James. 'So Barry and the boys left about an hour ago to cross the island to Black Hole Bay. I was telling them last night about the smugglers who used Merlin's Cave. It's near the bottom of the cliff in the bay. It can only be reached at low tide. We're wondering whether Hassin went to explore it.'

'Tommy and I will go around the island to the

bay,' said Robert. 'I hope we find him before it gets dark.'

'I'll come with you,' said Brother James. 'There is a dangerous reef called the Mare's Tail just off the bay. I know the channel.'

Brother James kept a sharp look-out for Hassin with his binoculars.

'Mare's Tail ahead!' he called suddenly. 'Keep Tommy out until I shout, then turn sharply inwards. The channel is shallow, but there is deep water inside the bay.'

The sea was foaming over the reef like soap-suds. Tommy went very slowly and carefully. Brother James was peering over his bows.

'Now!' shouted Brother James.

Robert spun the wheel. Tommy swung landwards. Below his keel was trailing seaweed and dark rocks. Suppose the water wasn't deep enough!

But, a few moments later, he was shore side of the reef. Black Hole Bay was large and round, with high cliffs, as though a giant had taken a bite out of the island.

'There are Barry and the boys!' exclaimed

Brother James. 'One of them is being lowered down the cliff-face. I think it's Billy.'

'Can you see Hassin?' asked Robert.

'No,' replied Brother James. 'But Flora is at the foot of the cliff and the waves are already washing around her hoofs.'

'Blistering Barnacles!' gasped Tommy. 'What has happened to him?'

'The entrance to Merlin's Cave is just above where Flora is standing,' explained Brother James. 'The cave is under that rock bulge. You can see the

ledge outside it. There's a steep slippery path up from the beach.'

'Billy must be going down to find out if Hassin is in the cave,' said Tommy. 'I do hope he is.'

Billy dropped farther and farther down the cliff. Suddenly, he stopped, his feet dangling just below the rock bulge, about three metres above the ledge.

'What's happened now?' asked Brother James.

'I think the rope is too short,' replied Robert. 'They'll have to pull him up again.'

But Billy didn't give up that easily. He wriggled

out of the loop on the end of the rope, and hung by his hands. He swung like a pendulum. When his feet were over the ledge, he let go, sprawling on hands and knees outside the mouth of the cave. He picked himself up, and disappeared into the cave.

Minutes passed. Suddenly, Billy appeared supporting Hassin. He tried to reach the dangling rope, but he wasn't tall enough. He climbed down to the beach. He plunged through the knee-deep sea to where Flora waited. He climbed up on her back, and tried to ride her up the path to the ledge. But Billy was no horseman. As Flora stumbled and slipped, he fell off backwards into the water.

'Tommy will have to go in,' cried Brother James. 'The tide is still rising. The cave could flood, and they could drown.'

Tommy was very scared that he would go aground, or be swept up against the cliff, but he knew that he had to try to save the boys and Flora. Robert steered him as near the beach as he dared. Brother James shouted to the boys through a loud-hailer.

'Billy! Help Hassin down to the beach. Hold on

to Flora's bridle tightly. I'll call her. Flora! Flora! Here girl!'

Luckily, both Billy and Hassin were good swimmers. When Flora heard Brother James's voice, she plunged into the sea. Billy and Hassin, holding the bridle in one hand and swimming with the other, were towed to Tommy. In a few moments, Robert and Brother James had hauled them aboard.

Robert dived overboard and fastened a webbing belt around Flora. Tommy lifted her with his derrick.

The boys were wet and cold, and Hassin had a sprained ankle, but otherwise they were unhurt.

Barry and the other boys came down to the jetty as Tommy moored there.

'Thank you very much, everyone,' said Hassin. 'Especially you, Billy and Tommy. You saved my life.'

'It was a smashing adventure!' cried Billy. 'Coo! Flora's a great swimmer.'

'She'll carry you both back to the farmhouse,' said Brother James. 'Dry clothes for you two. Supper and bed for you all.'

Robert and Tommy watched the procession slowly climbing the track. Brother James and Barry led Flora by the bridle. Hassin rode in front, and Billy clung to his waist. The rest of the boys walked beside them, joking and chattering.

'I think our Hassin has made some friends,' chuckled Robert.

5 *Tommy and Sea Giant*

The next few days, Hassin spent all his time with the boys. He worked hard, he swam and fished, and ate enormous meals. He taught the boys to snorkle, and Billy to ride. The two of them spent hours watching the gannets, and exploring the island.

But, if Tommy and Robert saw very little of Hassin, they saw lots of other people. The sale of Gannet Island had been advertised in the press.

Aberford fishermen brought boat loads of curious sight-seers. A fast speed-boat brought four business-men, who wanted to build a hotel and holiday camp on the island. A party of boat salesmen thought that if they installed lifts down the cliff, Black Hole Bay would make an ideal yacht marina. A group of Government Scientists decided that the old fort would make a research centre for rockets.

But what really upset Brother James, and terrified

his sea-birds, was the arrival by helicopter of American oil men. They proposed to blow up the Mare's Tail reef and use Black Hole Bay to build oil drilling platforms.

By Thursday evening, all the statues except King Arthur were in their wooden crates. Tommy left the island to deliver the last of them to Aberford. Brother James, Barry and Hassin went with him. Hassin wanted to telephone the Haven to find out when his father would be arriving.

When Tommy arrived in Aberford, Uncle Ben and most of his friends were on the quayside. They all agreed that they didn't want the island to become a yacht marina, or a holiday camp, or a rocket research centre. But, least of all, did they want the American oil men to buy it.

'My birds would lose their home,' cried Brother James.

'Everything would be changed,' said Uncle Ben. 'Not only the island, but Aberford, too.'

'It's such a shame,' cried Barry. 'The island would make an ideal place for an Adventure Centre. If only we had the money.'

'What's an Adventure Centre?' asked Robert.

'It's a place where boys and girls from the cities, who need space, freedom and fresh air, can spend their holidays,' explained Barry.

'That wouldn't spoil the island,' said Brother James.

'No,' agreed Barry. 'The farmhouse, and old fort could be used as living quarters. The young people could swim, fish, sail, watch birds, and see flowers and wild life.'

'Holidays like we're having?' asked Hassin.

'That's right,' replied Barry.

'It's a super idea,' cried Hassin. 'Then I could spend all my school holidays here. Why don't you buy Gannet Island at the Auction Sale on Saturday, Barry?'

'We couldn't afford to,' sighed Barry. 'The American oil men have so much money that they can out-bid everyone.'

'My father is rich,' said Hassin. 'Perhaps . . .'

But no one took any notice of the boy in grubby shorts. So he went off to telephone. The people talked and planned. But there seemed no way of

stopping the Americans buying Gannet Island.

On Friday morning, back on Gannet Island, King Arthur was put into his crate, and loaded on to Tommy's deck, beside his funnel.

'Thank you very much,' said Brother James.

'We're just finished in time,' said Barry. 'We go home on Sunday. What shall we do today, boys?'

'I have a plan,' said Hassin. 'The boys have never been on an oil tanker.'

'Neither have I,' said Barry.

'My father's largest tanker, Sea Giant, is arriving

this morning in the Haven,' explained Hassin. 'Her captain is a cousin of my mother. So, if Tommy could take us to the Haven, we would be most welcome on his ship.'

'Can you take us, Robert?' asked Barry.

'King Arthur will have to go too,' said Robert. 'We won't have time to go to Aberford first.'

The boys were very excited. Everyone helped to clear up. By noon, all was ship-shape. Tommy chugged away from the concrete jetty, and across the rumbling, tumbling sea. He passed the lighthouse, between the buoys, and up the Haven.

Sea Giant was moored at the end of a jetty. He *was* enormous. Tommy felt like a toy boat.

'Ahoy there, Sea Giant!' he tootled. 'I've brought someone to see you.'

'I'm afraid I'm rather busy,' hooted Sea Giant. 'I start to pump the oil from my hold through that pipe to the refinery in three hours' time.'

'Your visitors are Hassin, the son of Sheik Abdullah, and some of his friends,' explained Robert. 'Please tell your captain.'

When the sailors heard this, one of them jumped

on his bicycle, and rode off along the quarter-mile deck to fetch Captain Sadat.

Hassin, Barry, Robert and the boys climbed Tommy's gang-plank, and then several flights of iron stairs to the top of the jetty.

'Welcome to Sea Giant, Hassin,' called Captain Sadat, kissing him on both cheeks. 'I didn't expect you until tomorrow afternoon. Your father is not due to arrive here until tomorrow morning.'

'Can my friends look over Sea Giant?' asked Hassin. 'They've never been on a giant oil tanker.'

'Of course, Hassin,' said Captain Sadat. 'Come aboard.'

Captain Sadat told two of his sailors to take the visitors all over Sea Giant. By the time they had walked miles of passages, shot up and down in lifts, visited the engine-room, and seen the bridge, even the boys were tired. Barry and Robert were exhausted. But they all enjoyed a scrumptious tea in the captain's cabin.

At six o'clock, Robert said they must go. Barry thanked Captain Sadat for a wonderful afternoon.

'I'm going back to Gannet Island with my

friends,' said Hassin. 'Please tell my father that I must speak to him. It is most important. I will telephone him early tomorrow morning.'

'I will tell him,' promised Captain Sadat. 'Now, please excuse me. We are ready to start pumping our oil.'

Everyone went back aboard Tommy. Robert started his engine. A workman on the jetty cast off his mooring rope.

Suddenly, he heard a shout and a great splash.

'What the . . .' exclaimed Tommy. 'Blistering Barnacles! Look, Robert!'

A black wave of oil was flooding across Sea Giant's deck and down her side. A sailor watching the oil pipe slipped. In a few seconds, he was struggling in the water.

'We must try and save him,' cried Robert.

'He's swimming towards Sea Giant's bows,' yelled Barry.

'We must try and reach him between the jetty and the ship,' called Robert.

It was lucky that Tommy was small, and that the tide was low. He managed to squeeze under the

ironwork of the jetty, and to slither in beside Sea
Giant's bows.

The oil was pouring down the side of the ship
like a black waterfall. Tommy was scared. If Sea
Giant swung inwards, he would be crushed like an
egg-shell.

Barry stood on Tommy's bows. He threw a life-
belt to the sailor. Luckily, the man grabbed it
straight away. Barry and the boys were able to haul
him on deck. He was black with oil, and choking.
Tommy reversed quickly, and tied up again at the
jetty. Workmen wrapped the sailor in a blanket,

and carried him to the top of the jetty to wait for an ambulance.

Robert, Barry and the boys set to work with detergent, bucket and brush to clean the oil off Tommy's deck.

'What a mess!' exclaimed Robert, looking over Tommy's side.

The leaking valve in the pipe-line that had caused the trouble had been closed. But the oil that had already escaped was spreading across the Haven.

'It will kill the sea-birds and the fish, and spoil the beaches,' said Barry.

'Not if we can stop it.' A small boat about the size of Tommy, with the name Cleansea on its bows, came chugging up alongside. On its deck were drums of detergent, and coils of hosepipe. Attached to the end of each hose-pipe was a long metal nozzle, with holes in it. The nozzles fitted into special slots in the gunwale of Cleansea.

'What are you going to do?' asked Robert.

'Spray the oil,' answered the skipper. 'That's our job. We do our best to keep the water of the Haven clean.'

'Splendid work!' exclaimed Barry.

'It's very difficult with all these giant tankers unloading so much oil,' sighed the skipper. 'This is the second accident today.'

'Is there only one boat to spray the oil?' asked Tommy.

'There are usually two of us,' replied Cleansea. 'But my partner is working farther up the Haven. So I must do what I can here.'

'Can I help?' tootled Tommy.

'Yes, please,' answered the skipper. 'There are drums of detergent and hose-pipes on each jetty.

66

Could you load them, and just chug up and down with me, spraying the oil?'

For the next few hours, Tommy did just that. Because he had no slots in his gunwale, the boys manned the hose-pipes. The detergent sprayed out of the holes in the long metal nozzles on to the thick, black oil.

'It's just like watering the garden,' chuckled Barry.

At last, another boat like Cleansea came down the Haven.

'Thank you very much, Tommy,' said Cleansea. 'Here comes my partner. We'll be able to manage now. Where shall the Haven Office send your cheque, Robert?'

'Cheque!' repeated Robert. 'We don't want to be paid for helping you.'

'We enjoyed it,' tootled Tommy.

'You've worked for several hours,' said Cleansea. 'Ships who help us are always paid. Give it to someone who needs it if—'

'Martha!' exclaimed Tommy.

'Of course,' cried Robert. 'We'll start a Mend Martha Fund with your cheque. Could you send it to Ben Bowen's Boat Yard at Aberford, please?'

'Thank you very much,' said Barry.

'Cleansea,' said Robert. 'We have a derrick. Can we swing these drums and hose-pipes on to your deck please? It will save us going back to the jetty.'

'Of course,' said Cleansea. 'Follow me into shallower water near the shore, then we can both drop anchor.'

The hose-pipes and drums were swung on to Cleansea's deck. Robert and Barry were just handling the last full one, when it slipped. The rope hold it curled around King Arthur's crate. The statue fell sideways, and rolled. Splash! King Arthur had sunk below the water of the Haven.

'Glory be!' exclaimed Robert. 'We've lost King Arthur! What shall we tell Brother James?'

6 *Tommy helps a fishing boat*

Everyone was very upset at losing King Arthur. They peered down into the murky waters of the Haven. But they could see only a trail of bubbles, and a couple of broken pieces of the crate.

The skipper of Cleansea lent them a large orange buoy to mark the spot. Robert thought that the ship-building dock might know where they could hire a diver to find King Arthur. So Tommy chugged across the Haven.

But all the workmen had gone home. The watch-man said that he would try and find a diver for them next morning.

It was almost dark as Tommy chugged back to the oil refinery jetty, and tied up. The refinery towers were lit up like giant Christmas trees. Great arc lights shone on the jetty, and on Sea Giant's deck. The pumps throbbed as the oil flowed through the pipes. Everyone was much too busy to take notice of Tommy.

The boys had supper and a sing-song on deck. Then Robert lent each of them a blanket, and they slept wherever they could find a spare corner. Some were in deck-chairs, some in the engine-room, and one small boy curled up in a coil of rope.

They wakened very early next morning. Robert was frying a huge panful of sausages when he heard Hassin shout.

'It's my father!'

A taxi had stopped beside Sea Giant's gang-way. A tall man, wearing a white robe and head-dress had climbed out.

Hassin shot up Tommy's gang-plank, and raced up the iron stairs.

'Merciful Allah!' exclaimed Sheik Abdullah, as a boy in creased shorts hurled himself at him. 'Is this you, Hassin?'

Robert had turned off the gas ring. He and Barry had followed Hassin up the stairs. The Sheik held Hassin at arms' length.

'Can I believe my eyes?' asked the Sheik. 'I

expected a sick boy, who needed a sea voyage to make him well again!'

'Tommy and I did our best,' explained Robert. 'But, may I present Barry. It was he and his boys who really made Hassin well and happy.'

'I've had a super holiday on an island,' cried Hassin, 'and I've made new friends, and . . .'

'Then Allah be praised!' exclaimed the Sheik. 'You all have my deepest gratitude.'

'We helped to clean up an oil leak,' continued

Hassin, 'and we lost King Arthur overboard, and we're waiting for a skin diver, and . . .'

'Peace, boy! My mind is reeling,' chuckled the Sheik. 'What is all this talk of King Arthur?'

Robert explained what had happened.

'You shall have your diver,' promised the Sheik.

Sure enough, twenty minutes later, a rubber-clad skin diver came along the jetty. He was carrying his flippers and face-mask, and a cylinder of air called an aqualung.

'Robert, when you have rescued King Arthur, please bring Hassin back here,' said the Sheik. 'We are leaving for home tomorrow, so he can stay here tonight.'

'Oh no, Father,' protested Hassin. 'I want you to come to Aberford with Tommy today. We must be there by three o'clock. It's very important.'

'Oh, very well,' chuckled the Sheik. 'I'll hurry through my business here. When you come back, I'll be ready to come to Aberford with you. I do hope it is really important.'

'Oh, it is!' said Hassin.

When Tommy reached the orange buoy that

marked the spot where the statue had fallen over-board, the diver put on his flippers, mask and aqualung. He rolled backwards over Tommy's gunwale.

Everyone watched the trail of bubbles that showed where the diver was working. Presently, he came up. He trod water beside Tommy, and lifted his face-mask. He asked Robert to fasten a sling to the end of Tommy's cable. He lowered his face mask again, and holding the sling in one hand, he dived under the water. Everyone waited. Suddenly, he surfaced beside Tommy.

'Haul away!' he signalled.

Robert started Tommy's winch. Slowly and gently, Tommy pulled. Soon they could see the crate. Tommy's derrick lifted King Arthur back on deck. Barry helped the diver aboard. Robert and Barry examined the crate. A few slats had been broken, but, otherwise, it did not seem to be damaged.

Tommy chugged back to the jetty. Robert thanked the diver for his help, and the diver went away.

'I hope my father comes quickly,' said Hassin, looking at his watch. 'How long will it take Tommy to reach Aberford, Robert?'

'About three hours,' replied Robert.

Hassin ran up Tommy's gang-plank and raced up the iron stairs. When he returned, Sheik Abdullah was panting along behind him. A sailor from Sea Giant followed them. He handed a small suitcase to Robert, who was waiting to welcome the Sheik aboard.

'Cast off,' called Hassin to the sailor. 'Let's go, Robert.'

'You are in a hurry,' chuckled Robert.

Tommy tootled goodbye to Sea Giant, and chugged down the Haven.

'Please bring a deck-chair from the cabin to the bows, Billy,' said Hassin. 'Then take the other boys to the stern deck. I want to talk privately to my father.'

When Tommy reached the sea, the wind was blowing quite hard. The white-crested waves rolled and tumbled, and the spray was breaking over his bows.

Robert sent one of the boys along the deck with water-proof jackets, so that the Sheik and Hassin wouldn't get too wet. They talked for an hour.

The wind freshened, and it started to rain. Everyone had to shelter in Tommy's cabin. His engine pounded and thumped as he ploughed through the rough sea. But he was making good time. By one o'clock, he had almost reached the Cat and Kittens rocks.

Suddenly, up ahead, a rocket shot into the air, exploding into three red stars that hung for a few seconds in the cloudy sky.

'Someone in trouble, Robert!' tootled Tommy.

Robert steered Tommy towards the place where they had seen the rocket. In the driving rain, they could only see a short distance, so they chugged around in circles, searching and looking. At last, they spotted an open fishing boat, wallowing and rolling in the waves. As Tommy came closer, they could see a small, slight figure in yellow oil-skins in the cockpit. Tommy tootled his tooter.

'Ahoy there! Are you in danger?' called Robert.

'Oh, yes! Please help me!' wailed the figure.

'Good gracious!' exclaimed Barry. 'I think it's a girl!'

'A huge wave broke over our stern,' called the girl. 'It swept my father along the deck. He's broken his leg. The engine stalled, and I can't start it again. So the pumps aren't working, and we're half full of water.'

'Someone will have to go aboard, and help her,' decided Robert.

Barry offered to go. The boys fastened a rope around his waist, and held tightly to the end.

It was a difficult manoeuvre. Three times,

77

Robert tried to steer Tommy in beside the rolling, helpless fishing boat. Each time, the waves swept them apart.

The fourth time, Robert managed to put Tommy almost alongside. Barry leapt. A wave lifted the launch. The rope around Barry's waist snaked through the boys' hands. But Barry managed to grab the gunwale. For a few seconds, he hung on grimly, as the wave washed over him. Then, the girl reached over, and dragged him on to the deck.

He clambered to his feet, and climbed down into

78

the cockpit. Everyone waited. Tommy's engines thudded as Robert held his bows towards the rolling waves. Anxious moments passed.

Barry reappeared.

'It's no use,' he shouted. 'I can't start the engine. You'll have to give us a tow.'

Billy and Hassin helped to hold Tommy steady, while Robert fired the thin line across to Barry. Several times, the wind caught it, and it dropped in the sea. But, at last, Barry managed to catch it. He and the girl pulled Tommy's heavy rope across and fastened it to the bows of the fishing boat.

'Best screw forward, now Tommy!' shouted Barry. 'Our injured man should be in hospital.'

Tommy started to tow. The fishing boat was almost full of water, so it was heavy. It wallowed and yawed behind him, swinging his stern from side to side. Soon, the rain stopped, the wind began to die down, and the sun came out. Tommy pulled as hard as he could, but he was still travelling very slowly.

Hassin kept looking at his watch as the minutes ticked by. Two o'clock! A quarter past! They'd never reach Aberford in time!

7   *A happy ending after all*

Hassin was very upset. The Sheik was just trying to console him, when they heard the sound of an engine. A helicopter hovered over them.

'Ahoy there!' called the pilot. 'The coastguard radioed that he had seen a rocket just after one o'clock. Did either of you fire it?'

'Yes, I did,' shouted the girl. 'But Tommy found me, and he's helping me.'

'If you have everything under control, we'll go back to our base,' called the pilot.

'Wait!' shouted Barry. 'We have a man aboard with a broken leg. Can you help him?'

'We can take him to Aberford Cottage Hospital,' replied the pilot.

'Do you have room for me, too?' called Sheik Abdullah. 'This rescue has delayed me. I *must* be in Aberford before three o'clock.'

The pilot was only too happy to help. He lowered a stretcher. Barry and the girl fastened the injured man to it. He was winched up into the helicopter. Then the Sheik was hauled up in a rescue sling. The helicopter flew away towards Aberford.

It was four o'clock when Tommy towed the swamped fishing boat up the deep, narrow creek, and beached it. He tied up beside Martha. Brother James's motor-boat was moored behind her. The girl thanked them, and went off to the hospital to see her father.

The quay was crowded with people. The businessmen, the boat salesmen, the Government Scientists, and the American oil men were all there.

'Of course!' exclaimed Robert. 'It's the auction sale for Gannet Island! I'd forgotten it.'

'I hadn't!' said Hassin.

Brother James and Uncle Ben came along the quay. Hassin and the boys shot up Tommy's gangplank.

'Brother James!' yelled Hassin. 'Who bought Gannet Island? Did my father come?'

'A fine looking Arab gentleman arrived by helicopter about ten minutes before the sale,' chuckled Brother James. 'I think he's inside the Lobster Pot Inn.'

Hassin and the boys ran along the quay and pushed their way into the inn. Robert and Barry fastened the derrick to King Arthur, and swung him on to the quay. Brother James was inspecting him when Sheik Abdullah and the boys came back.

'Well, my friends,' said the Sheik, taking Hassin by the hand, 'behold the new owner of Gannet Island.'

'You, Hassin!' exclaimed Brother James. 'Why?'

'I've been so happy there,' replied Hassin. 'Now I can spend all my holidays on the island.'

'Oh! I see,' said Barry sadly.

'No, I see that you do not understand,' chuckled the Sheik. 'The island belongs to Hassin. But he wants to help you make it an Adventure Centre for your boys and girls. You can rent it for the next twenty years. At . . . um . . . one pound per year?'

Everyone was so excited. Barry led the boys in three cheers for the Sheik and Hassin.

'We take over the island when Brother James

leaves on the first of August,' explained the Sheik.
'So some of your boys and girls can have a holiday
this summer.'

'How will they get to the island?' asked Robert.
'When we have taken the Sheik and Hassin back
to the Haven, we leave for Spedemouth.'

'My boat has already been sold,' said Brother
James.

'I have to take visitors on fishing trips,' added
Uncle Ben.

84

'Couldn't I do it?' pleaded Martha. 'I'm old, but I'm a sturdy boat. If I was repaired . . .'

'Oh Martha, I'm sorry!' cried Tommy. 'In all the excitement about the island, I forgot to tell you. We're putting our cheque from the Haven Board into a Mend Martha Fund.'

'What is this Mend Martha Fund?' asked the Sheik.

Robert explained about the repairs and the new engine that Martha needed. Brother James offered to add to the fund the money from the sale of his boat. Barry and the boys planned to do lots of odd jobs in Birmingham, and give the money to the fund.

'Father! We must help too,' said Hassin.

'Of course,' agreed the Sheik. 'I owe you a great debt, Tommy and Robert, for what you have done for my son. So, my agent in the Haven will arrange delivery of a new engine for Martha.'

When the boys heard this, they cheered again.

Uncle Ben promised to start work on the urgent repairs straight away, so that Martha would, at least, be seaworthy by the first of August. He also agreed that, later on, he would teach Barry and the boys and girls to renovate and refit Martha so that she would be as strong and beautiful as the day she was built.

Then, Hassin asked Brother James about Flora. When he heard she was to stay on the island, he offered to care for her for the rest of the summer.

'But you were coming back to Saudi Arabia with me, tomorrow,' cried Sheik Abdullah.

'Not now, father,' said Hassin. 'I must stay on

my island. Barry will be back on the first of August with more new friends for me. I want to help repair Martha, too.'

'You can stay with me in the farmhouse until then,' suggested Brother James.

'Or over here with me,' added Uncle Ben.

'That seems to be nicely settled,' said the Sheik. 'I shall stay in the hotel at Aberford, and fly home next week. I'd like to visit this marvellous island.'

'It's a super place, father,' cried Hassin. 'It's got . . .'

'Later!' chuckled the Sheik. 'Now you are all to come to the Lobster Pot Inn for a meal. We'll have fresh Welsh lobsters, and ice–cream, and whatever else you fancy.'

The Sheik led the way along the quay. Hassin and the boys ran beside him. Brother James, Uncle Ben and Barry followed.

Tommy and Martha were left beside the jetty.

'Thank you, Tommy,' said Martha. 'It's a happy ending for everyone after all.'

'Yes, it is,' tootled Tommy happily. 'We've had

a very exciting holiday, too. I'm glad we came to Wales again.'

'So are many other people!' said Martha.

Further adventures with Tommy the Tugboat

TOMMY THE TUGBOAT

TOMMY JOINS THE NAVY

TOMMY GETS A MEDAL

FERRYBOAT TOMMY

TOMMY'S NEW ENGINE

TOMMY AND THE ONION BOAT

TOMMY AND THE OIL RIG

TOMMY AND THE LIGHTHOUSE

TOMMY AND THE SPANISH GALLEON

TOMMY AND THE YELLOW SUBMARINE

TOMMY IN THE CARIBBEAN